TUSK! TUSK!

written and illustrated by

ANNIE MITRA

Holiday House/New York

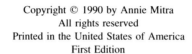

Library of Congress Cataloging-in-Publication Data

Mitra, Annie.
Tusk! tusk! / written and illustrated by Annie Mitra.—1st ed.
p.   cm.
Summary: Waking up on his birthday with a toothache, Elephant
visits the dentist and learns about proper tooth care.
ISBN 0-8234-0819-1
[1. Teeth—Care and hygiene—Fiction. 2. Dental care—Fiction.
3. Elephants—Fiction.]   I. Title.
PZ7.M69955Tu   1990
[E]—dc20   89-77508   CIP   AC
ISBN 0-8234-0819-1

An elephant without tusks is like a leopard without spots.

When Elephant woke up on his birthday,
he was very unhappy.
"My tooth hurts," he said.
He went back to bed with
a cup of tea and a bucket of jelly beans.

Elephant was still in bed when
his friend Alligator arrived.
''Happy Birthday!'' cried Alligator.
But Elephant didn't answer.
''What's the matter?'' asked Alligator.
''I've got a toothache,'' replied Elephant.

"Well then, we had better
  make you better!" said Alligator.
"Let's go to the dentist."
"But what about my birthday party?" asked Elephant.
"Your party is not till later," said Alligator.

Elephant and Alligator went to the dentist.
When they arrived, they had to wait
in line like everybody else.

"What's wrong with you, Rhino?" asked Elephant.

"I've got a new tooth," replied Rhino.

"I've got a loose tooth," said Rabbit.

"And I haven't got a single tooth!" squawked Rooster.

"Who's next?" asked the dentist.

Soon, it was Elephant's turn.

"What can I do for you?" asked the dentist.

"I've got an awful toothache," said Elephant.

"Well, sit down and let me have a look.

Tsk! Tsk! What have we here?" said the dentist.

"Jelly beans." He sighed.

"Far too many jelly beans. You have a cavity . . ."

Elephant blushed.

''If you're not careful, you will be like Lion.
  He had a mouth *full* of cavities,'' said the dentist.
''They hurt so much that he couldn't roar.''

"Or like Warthog, who ate so much candy that his teeth fell out!"

"Or like Crocodile, who wouldn't smile
  because he never brushed his teeth
  and they were rotten."

''And poor Fish had to have *false* teeth,
which made it very hard to chew . . .

"Oh dear," said Elephant,
"how should I take care of my teeth, then?"
"It's easy," said the dentist.
"Just brush and floss your teeth *every* day."
"Is that all?" asked Elephant.

"No, you also have to keep the cavities away.
That means not too much sugar, and certainly
not too many jelly beans."
"Does that mean I can't have
my birthday party?" asked Elephant.

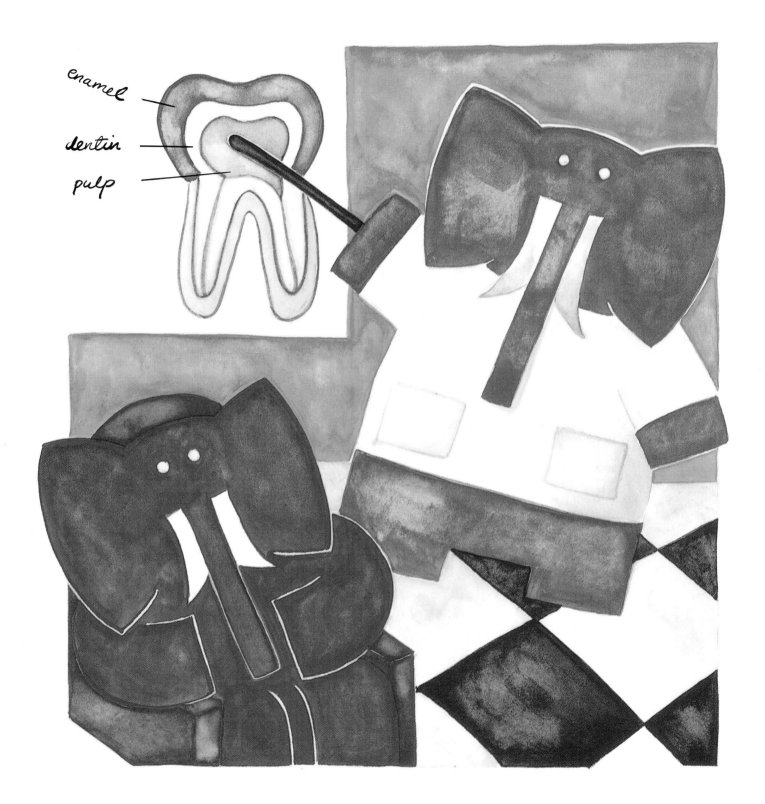

enamel

dentin

pulp

"Of course you can have your party,"
  replied the dentist.
"Just try munching and crunching!

Munch on apples and crunch on carrots.
Rabbits crunch on carrots to keep
their teeth nice and white.''

"What else should I eat?" asked Elephant.

"Milk and cheese are good for your teeth, too."

"All right," sighed Elephant,

"but what about my toothache?"

"Open wide," said the dentist.

The dentist filled Elephant's cavity
and gave him a new blue toothbrush.

"Thank you," said Elephant.

"Come back and see me soon," said the dentist.

"May we go now?" asked Alligator.
Elephant and Alligator ran home
and prepared for the party.
They made a huge birthday cake,
—and they also remembered what
the dentist had told them.

Elephant's friends soon arrived.
"Happy Birthday!" they shouted.
Alligator did some magic tricks,
and Elephant blew out the candles.

When the party was over,
Elephant brushed and flossed his teeth
and went to bed.